Bounce,
Tigger,
Bounce!

Disney's
Winnie the Pooh First Readers

Be Quiet, Pooh!
Bounce, Tigger, Bounce
The Giving Bear
Happy Birthday, Eeyore!
Pooh's Christmas Gifts
Pooh's Fall Harvest
Pooh's Graduation
Pooh's Halloween Parade
Pooh's Leaf Pile
Pooh's Pumpkin
Pooh's Scavenger Hunt
Pooh's Sled Ride
Pooh and the Storm That Sparkled
Pooh's Surprise Basket
Rabbit Gets Lost
Tiggers Hate to Lose
World's Best Mama

DISNEY's

A Winnie the Pooh First Reader

Bounce, Tigger, Bounce!

Isabel Gaines

Illustrated by Francesc Rigol

Random House 🏠 New York

Library of Congress Control Number: 00-108677
ISBN: 0-7364-1141-0 (paperback)

First Random House Edition January 2001 Printed in the United States of America 10 9 8

www.randomhouse.com/kids/disney

Bounce, Tigger, Bounce!

Roo was waiting for Tigger.

He was beginning to think

Tigger would *never* come.

Just then, Tigger

bounced up the path.

He bounced so hard a big blob

of snow fell off the roof.

PLOP!

It landed on Roo's head.

"Hi, little buddy," Tigger said.

"Are you ready to go bouncing?"

"I am! I am!" Roo cried.

And off they went.

8

Tigger took big bounces, like this:

BOING! BOING! BOING!

Roo took little ones, like this:

BOING! BOING! BOING!

Tigger and Roo bounced

deeper into the woods.

Soon they came to a tall tree.

Roo looked way up

into the branches.

"Can Tiggers climb trees?"

he asked.

"Climbing trees is what Tiggers

do best," said Tigger.

"Only they don't just climb them.

They *bounce* them!

Here . . . I'll show you."

Tigger bent down, and Roo
hopped onto his shoulders.
Up the tree they bounced.
BOING! BOING! BOING!

Soon they reached
the very top.
Tigger looked down.
His head began to spin.

13

Suddenly, Tigger's tail

felt funny, too.

Roo was swinging

back and forth on it.

"S-s-stop that," Tigger begged.

"You're rocking the forest."

14

Just then,

Pooh and Piglet came by.

"HELP!" Tigger yelled down.

"Tigger!" Pooh yelled up.

"And Roo!

What are you doing up there?"

"Tigger is stuck," said Roo.

15

Pooh and Piglet hurried off
to get some help.
They came right back
with Kanga, Rabbit, and
Christopher Robin.

16

"Tigger is stuck," Roo

told his mother.

"That's too bad," she said.

"No, it's good," Rabbit said.

"Tigger can't bounce anyone

up there!"

"Well," said Christopher Robin,

"we have to get them *both* down."

17

Christopher Robin took off
his coat.
Pooh grabbed a corner.

18

"Here I come!" cried Roo.

"WHEEEE!"

He jumped right into the coat.

Then it was Tigger's turn.

"Jump, Tigger!" said
Christopher Robin.
"Tiggers don't jump,"
said Tigger. "They bounce."

"Then you'll have to climb down,"

said Christopher Robin.

"Tiggers *can't* climb down," said Tigger.

"Their tails get in the way."

And he wrapped his tail tightly

around the tree trunk.

21

"If I ever get down,"
Tigger gasped,
"I promise never
to bounce again!"
Rabbit's ears snapped
straight up.
"I heard that!" he cried.

Well, it took a while.

But not forever.

Tigger didn't jump down.

And he didn't climb down.

He just unwrapped his tail

and slo-o-owly slid down the tree.

PLOP!

Tigger landed in the soft snow.

He was so happy to be back

down, he felt like bouncing.

"No, no, no!" Rabbit cried.

"You promised. No bouncing!"

"You mean I can't *ever* bounce again?"

"Never," Rabbit said.

"Not even one teensy-weensy

bounce?" Tigger asked.

"Not even one," Rabbit replied.

Tigger's chin dropped.

His tail drooped.

Sadly he turned away.

Tigger's friends stared after him.

They all felt sad, too.

Except for Rabbit.

He was smiling.

Roo looked from Rabbit
to Tigger and back again.
"I like the old bouncy Tigger
best," he said at last.
"Me, too," everyone else said.
Everyone but Rabbit.

"What about you, Rabbit?"
said Kanga.

"Well," said Rabbit. "I . . . ah . . .
I . . . that is, I . . ."

For once, Rabbit didn't know
what to say.

Rabbit thought about all
the times Tigger had bounced him.
Then he thought about how sad
Tigger seemed without his bounce.
"Oh, all right," he finally said.
"I guess I like the old Tigger
better, too."

Before Rabbit could change

his mind, Tigger said,

"Come on, Rabbit.

Let's you and me bounce."

31

"Me bounce?" Rabbit said.

"Why not?" Tigger said.

"You have the feet for it."

Rabbit looked down

at his big, flat feet.

"I have?" he said.

"You have!" everyone

else agreed.

Rabbit tried a little bounce.

BOING!

Then he tried a bigger one.

BOING!

Soon he was bouncing

just like Tigger.

33

"Come on," Rabbit cried.

"Everybody bounce!"

And so they did.

They all bounced

together through

the Hundred-Acre Wood!